Mr Grinling was a lighthouse keeper. He and Mrs Grinling lived with their cat, Hamish, in the little white cottage perched high on the cliffs.

It was nearly Christmas and Mr Grinling's great-nephew, George, was coming to stay.

"We'll make it the best Christmas ever for George and for you," said Mrs Grinling as she bustled around the kitchen.

Mr Grinling sighed. "Sometimes I forget it's my last Christmas as the lighthouse keeper."

"Perhaps we could have Christmas Day in the lighthouse," suggested Mrs Grinling.

"Mrs G, I think that's the best idea you've ever had. Christmas Day in my lighthouse, how perfectly splendid."

George arrived.

"Wowee," he exclaimed. "Christmas Day in the lighthouse."

"I must write to Father Christmas so he knows where I am. Can you help me please, Uncle G?" he asked.

They wrote the letter together.

Dear FATHER
CHRISTMAS.
I will be at the
Grinlings' house on
Christmas eve.
They have a chimney.
Your friend,
George.

"What is Father Christmas
bringing you, Uncle G?"
asked George.

"I've suggested a lovely
pair of fluffy slippers," said
Mrs Grinling.

Mr Grinling was horrified.
"Slippers for Christmas!
What a boring present."

Dear FATHER CHRISTMAS,
Uncle G says that he would
like something for
christmas that's fun
to wear.
No boring slippers.
Your friends,
Mr Grinling and George
P.S. Hamish would like
another toy mouse

On Christmas Eve, Mrs Grinling was so busy that Mr Grinling and George had to make their own lunch.

They packed everything into the boat and rowed out to the lighthouse.

"See you tonight," called Mrs Grinling. "Don't be late."

There was lots to do.

Mr Grinling cleaned,

George polished,

and Hamish slept.

At last the lighthouse shone like a new pin.

"George," said Mr Grinling, "you're the best lighthouse helper I've ever had. I think you've earned yourself a splendiferous lunch."

They sat outside in the wintry sunshine. A lone grey seal basked nearby.

"I wish I could help at the lighthouse all the time," said George. "Will you be sad when you're not a lighthouse keeper any more?"

"Yes and no," said Mr Grinling. "On the days when the wind howls each way, every way, and my fingers are so cold I can't even feel them, then I won't be sad. But on the other days, when the sun shines and little boats frolic on that blue sea – yes, George, then I will be sad. But Sam is looking after the lighthouse so I can come and visit whenever I like."

Later, they put up the Christmas decorations and sang Christmas carols together, very loudly.

They were so busy that Mr Grinling didn't notice the darkening sky.

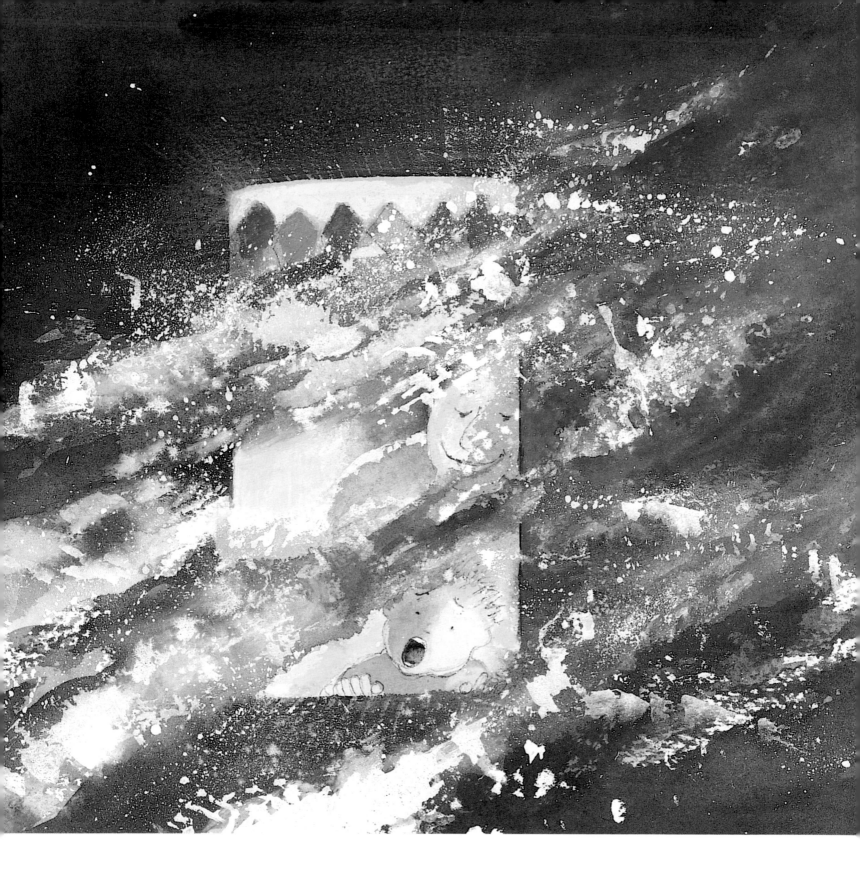

A wave splashed the window. "What's that?" asked George.
"Well, well," said Mr Grinling, "I think we're in for a storm."
"I don't like storms," said George. "Could we go home now, please?"

But when they opened the lighthouse door they could see the little dinghy tossed high by the waves. Mr Grinling tried to reach it with the boat hook but the dinghy was too far away.

George began to cry.

"Now George," said Mr Grinling. "No tears. We've got plenty of water already. You're a very lucky boy."

George stopped crying. "Am I?" he said.

"Absolutely," announced Mr Grinling. "You're probably the luckiest boy in the whole world because you're in the middle of a Christmas Eve Lighthouse Adventure. As a special treat you can turn on the light."

George cheered up enough to feel hungry.

"Do people have tea when they're in the middle of an adventure?"

Well done, George!

Mr Grinling rummaged in the lunch basket. It was quite empty.

"They do," he said. "But they ring Mrs Grinling first."

The wind was so fierce that George and
Mr Grinling tied themselves to the rail as
they waited for the food basket to arrive
in the usual way.

It turned and twisted down the wire. But the wind was hungry too. With an almighty gust it threw the basket high in the air.

The lid dropped open and George and Mr Grinling watched the seagulls dive on their tea as it fell to the ground.

"Never mind," said Mr Grinling. "There must be something in the cupboard.
I'll see what I can rustle up."

He found a very small tin of baked beans, some sardines, one shrivelled
potato and a packet of chocolate biscuits.

"What a feast," he declared. "Just right for a Christmas Eve adventure."

After they'd eaten, Mr Grinling made up some beds. Still the wind howled, still the waves roared, and thunder clouds filled the air.

"Listen to that weather," said Mr Grinling. "This adventure is getting more exciting all the time."

"I always have a story before I go to sleep, Uncle G," said George.

"Of course," said Mr Grinling. "Now let me see. I know, I'll tell you about the time when Father Christmas forgot to come to our house on Christmas Eve."

Oh dear!

George leapt out of bed.

"Oh no," he cried. "Father Christmas doesn't know that we're stranded in the lighthouse tonight. He'll take our presents to the little white cottage. What shall we do?"

Mr Grinling found a pen and some paper and together they wrote a very large notice for Father Christmas.

They attached it to the top lighthouse window. Every time the light flashed to the east it lit up the notice.

FATHER CHRISTMAS, FATHER CHRISTMAS.
WE ARE AT THE LIGHTHOUSE TONIGHT.
PLEASE ASK THE REINDEER TO BRING THE
SLEIGH TO THE DOOR BECAUSE THERE ISN'T
ANY CHIMNEY.   YOUR FRIENDS
GEORGE AND Mr GRINLING AND HAMISH

"Are you absolutely certain that Father Christmas will see it?" asked George anxiously.

"I am absolutely certain, George," reassured Mr Grinling.

"But what about our Christmas stockings?" asked George.

"Mmmm," mused Mr Grinling. "If I can just remember where
I put them . . ."

He found two enormous yellow socks.

"I knitted these myself."

They left the socks and a chocolate biscuit by the lighthouse door,
then Mr Grinling tucked George back into bed.

George woke in the middle of the night. Outside, the world was quiet and still again. Except for a slight tinkling noise.

He tip-toed to the window. It was the night before Christmas, and the moon shone dark in the sky.

"You found us, Father Christmas," he whispered.

George was first up in the morning. He and Hamish peered out of the window. Snow lay all around, even on the grey seals.

"Wowee," George exclaimed. "It's a proper Christmas after all, presents AND snow."

Then George's face dropped.

"I can't see the little white cottage, or the path. They're covered in snow. Maybe Auntie G is stranded now. How will she get to us for Christmas?"

"Goodness gracious me, George, don't you worry," chuckled Mr Grinling. "Mrs G is full of good ideas. I'm sure she'll think of something, just you wait and see."

They had two chocolate biscuits each for breakfast while they opened some of their presents.

At last Mrs Grinling rang.
"As it's your final meal
as the lighthouse keeper,
I'm sending Christmas
dinner in the basket.
Don't worry about me,
I'll get there somehow."
"Mrs G, you're wonderful,"
grinned Mr Grinling.

George and Mr Grinling waited patiently
as the basket slid down the wire.

George shook his fist at the scavenging
seagulls. "Clear off, you pesky birds!
Leave our Christmas dinner alone."

The basket stopped. Mr Grinling shook
the wire but the basket wouldn't move.

His tummy rumbled. He was sure he
could smell roast potatoes.

It's his last
Christmas, Bert!

Shall we
help?

Oh dear, Fred.
That dinner
is stuck!

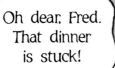

Tom, Bert and Fred hovered above the basket.
"No, no, no!" shouted George and Mr Grinling. But the seagulls
ignored them.
"Squawk, squawk!" they cried, and all together they dived.
The basket jerked and wobbled, then slid down the wire.

Dive, dive, dive!

Altogether now,
boys

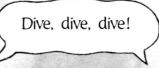

"Well I never," exclaimed
Mr Grinling. "Those
seagulls, they're full of
surprises."

George and Mr Grinling unpacked the Christmas dinner.
"Look," said Mr Grinling. "Mrs G has sent some little extra food packets." He read the labels. "Happy Christmas to those pesky seagulls, Tom, Bert and Fred."

TOM

BERT

A speedboat circled the lighthouse.
George waved and called.
   "Uncle G, Uncle G, it's alright!
Auntie G is here and Sam's come too."
   "I knew she'd get here somehow,"
smiled Mr Grinling.

Sam was carrying a large sack.
"More presents," he said, "from
all the people in the village."

And he read from the biggest card
Mr Grinling had ever seen.
"Happy retirement to the best
lighthouse keeper in the world."

Mr Grinling wiped his right eye.

"Now, now, Uncle G," said George
firmly. "No tears. We've got plenty
of water already."

"Quite right, George," said
Mr Grinling. "This is no time to
be sad. You and I have had the
best Christmas lighthouse
adventure ever."

"And now we're going to have
the best Christmas dinner ever,"
said Mrs Grinling.

It was almost dark by the time they finished eating.

"Time for your last light, Mr G," announced Sam.

"Come on everybody," said Mr Grinling. "Let's turn it on together."

The light beamed brightly and clearly out to sea. From out of the darkness all around came the sound of hooting and tooting from the ships and boats.

"That's the best present a lighthouse keeper could have," said Mr Grinling. "Thank you, thank you everybody."